To:
Gage :)
Have fun with Theodore!
Dave Gregory
2003

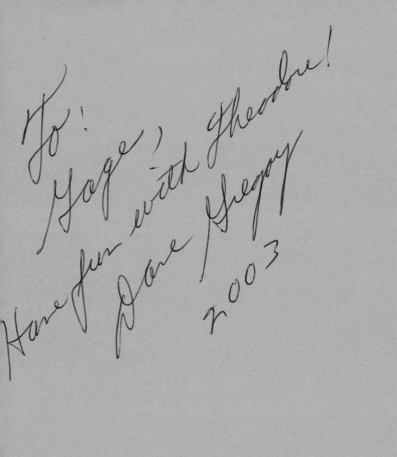

THEODORE WAS HERE

This Book Belongs To

_____

Thanks to Mike Hulme, graphic artist, for
creating Theodore and believing in the song and story.

Thanks to our families for all their support
and encouragement.

— **The Authors**

For my Mom and Dad,

— **Vuthy Kuon**

Copyright © 1997 by Dave Gregory
All rights reserved.
Published by Theodore Publishing Inc.
P.O.Box 381812, Duncanville, TX 75138
For ordering information, call (972)298-0214
Printed in Hong Kong by Paramount Printing
Second Printing 10 9 8 7 6 5 4 3
Book Design by Kris Park

Library of Congress Catalog Card Number 96-90451
Gregory/Puls, Theodore Was Here
Summary: Christmas elf named Theodore is Santa's
brand new helper. Theodore makes humorous mis-
takes as he helps Santa deliver toys on Christmas Eve.
ISBN 0-9653798-0-9

THEODOR WAS HERE

Written by

DAVE GREGORY & GRACE PULS

Illustrated by

VUTHY KUON

THEODORE PUBLISHING

DUNCANVILLE

Christmas time is here again
with Santa in a whirl.
'Twas time to make that yearly
trip to every boy and girl.

Santa asked for helpers to complete

that mighty chore.

Of all the elves that did apply...

He Chose Theodore!

Santa's brand new helper had

finished his first run,

and Santa had to laugh at what

Theodore had done.

He tied tin cans to Blitzen's tail

when he refused to fly,

and the **clink clank clink** and

the **plink plank plink**

could be heard across the sky.

He grabbed a jar of magic soap

from a bag that sat nearby,

and with a **huff huff huff**

and a **puff puff puff**

blew bubbles through the sky.

He came down through a chimney
with the toys in Santa's sack,
and with a **bump bump bump** and
a **thump thump thump**,
he landed on his back.

He went to every home that night,

but listen if you please.

Just when he should be so quiet

was when he had to sneeze!

He took a gun to all the girls

and a doll to all the boys...

...and with a **lick lick lick**

on a peppermint stick,

he made an awful noise!

He flipped the switch on the 'lectric train and didn't know what to do, and a **toot toot toot** and a **choo choo choo** put Theodore in a stew.

He wound each clock on the mantel

shelf before he rode away,

and the **tick tick tick** and

the **tock tock tock**

said, "Time for Christmas day!"

He went to every home that night

and shouted loud and clear

as he drove away in his jingling sleigh,

"Theodore was here!"

He left so many chuckles across

this weary land that

Theodore forevermore will be

Santa's right-hand man.